ARE THEY REAL?

ZOMBIES AND THE UNDEAD

by Emma Kaiser

BrightPoint Press

San Diego, CA

LIBRARY OF CONGRESS CATALOGING-IN-PUBLICATION DATA

Names: Kaiser, Emma, 1996--author.
Title: Zombies and the undead / by Emma Kaiser.
Description: San Diego, CA: BrightPoint Press, [2024] | Series: Are they real? | Includes
  bibliographical references and index. | Audience: Ages 13 | Audience: Grades 7-9
Identifiers: LCCN 2023000079 (print) | LCCN 2023000080 (eBook) | ISBN 9781678206406
  (hardcover) | ISBN 9781678206413 (eBook)
Subjects: LCSH: Zombies--Juvenile literature.
Classification: LCC GR581 .K34 2024 (print) | LCC GR581 (eBook) | DDC 398.21--dc23/
  eng/20230113
LC record available at https://lccn.loc.gov/2023000079
LC eBook record available at https://lccn.loc.gov/2023000080

CONTENTS

AT A GLANCE

- A zombie is a body that rises from the dead. It is driven by the need to bite or feed on the living.

- Zombies can be created through curses, spells, infections, or supernatural events.

- Cutting off a zombie's head is one of the only ways to stop it.

- The original idea of zombies comes from Haitian voodoo folklore. A voodoo priest is said to raise people back from the dead as slaves.

- The modern zombie that most people recognize comes from the 1968 George Romero film *Night of the Living Dead*.

- There are cases of humans and animals having zombielike symptoms. These can come from infections, poisonous toxins, or mental illnesses.

- There are some reports of people appearing to come back from the dead.

- Zombies are incredibly popular monsters in modern media. They are often featured in movies, television shows, and video games.

- Zombies are a reflection of very real human fears. But there is no evidence for zombies existing in real life.

INTRODUCTION

BACK FROM THE DEAD?

A man named Dylan walked down the street one evening. It started to get a little dark outside. The streetlights turned on. A gust of wind blew some leaves across the sidewalk. A full moon was shining in the sky. Dylan walked past a graveyard with a tall iron gate.

Suddenly, Dylan heard moaning. He turned the corner. There was a group of people in the distance. But they were acting weird. They were shuffling and dragging their feet. Their heads tilted to the side.

Some zombies are created by bringing the dead back to life.

Zombies are more dangerous in groups than they are by themselves.

Some of their arms hung limp. Some had

bodies bent at weird angles.

The **mob** of people started coming

toward Dylan. As they got closer, he

saw their clothes were dirty and ripped.

There was a dark liquid on their clothes and skin. It almost looked like blood. The people's faces were pale. Their eyes were unfocused.

The mob seemed to be getting bigger. They started reaching toward Dylan. They looked like they were coming right at him. Their mouths were open. The creatures almost looked hungry. Dylan wondered if he should turn and run. But his feet felt frozen to the ground.

The creatures surrounded Dylan. They were just about to grab him! Suddenly, a man sitting in a director's chair yelled out,

"Cut!" The creatures stopped. They started to stand up straight and walk normally. Some stood to the side and talked. Some walked over to a table to grab a snack. Dylan breathed a huge sigh of relief.

Dylan knew the zombies were not real. They were just actors making a movie. But even if they were not real, they were still scary.

MYTH OR REALITY?

Some call them the undead or the walking dead. Some call them living corpses. Whatever they are called, zombies are some

Movies, television shows, and video games are some of the most popular forms of zombie media.

of the most well-known monsters around today. They have become a big part of modern culture. Popular media has shown how scary these flesh-eating monsters can be. But do zombies really exist?

1

WHAT IS A ZOMBIE?

A zombie is a body that rises from the dead. It seems to come back to life. But zombies are not actually alive. They do not act the way people do. Some zombies only shuffle around mindlessly. Sometimes they can run. And they only want to feed on human flesh.

These undead monsters are often created through spells, infections, or **supernatural** events. After this happens, they look for people and eat them alive. Zombies can turn living people into more

Since zombies never get tired and do not need sleep, they never stop looking for flesh to eat.

zombies by biting them. This lets zombies quickly spread around the world.

Zombies look like dead bodies. Their skin might be rotting. They might be bloody or have open wounds. They might be missing body parts. They even continue to **decay** like a dead body would.

ZOMBIE CHARACTERISTICS

Part of what makes a zombie dangerous is that it is already dead. This means it does not feel pain. It does not feel fear either. Zombies cannot die the way a human can. Wounding a zombie might slow it down.

PARTS OF A ZOMBIE

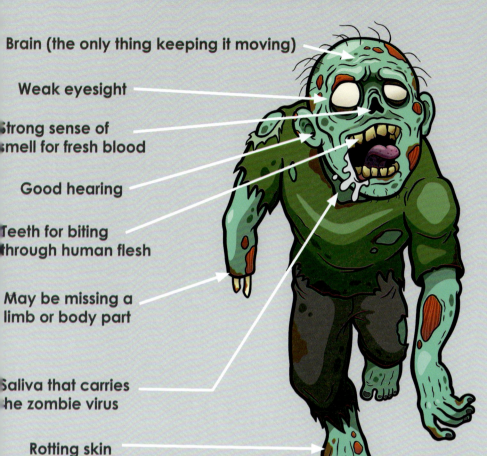

Brain (the only thing keeping it moving)

Weak eyesight

Strong sense of smell for fresh blood

Good hearing

Teeth for biting through human flesh

May be missing a limb or body part

Saliva that carries the zombie virus

Rotting skin

Zombies used to be living people. But after they are infected, the person begins to look like a walking corpse.

But the wound does not kill it. Sometimes a

zombie's disconnected arm will even keep

moving on its own. The only way to truly stop a zombie is by destroying the brain.

Zombies are not very smart or aware. They also do not talk like people do. Instead, they growl, grunt, moan, or scream. They do not need sleep and never get tired. Zombies also do not see very well. But they have great hearing and smell. Loud noises and the smell of blood will draw them in.

JIANG SHI

In China, *Jiang Shi* means stiff corpse. It is known in Chinese **folklore** as a hungry ghost. Jiang Shi come back to attack the living. A person must be buried properly so they can pass safely into the afterlife. If not, they will come back as a Jiang Shi.

Newer zombies are usually stronger than older zombies. This is because newer zombies are not as decayed as the older ones are.

Zombies become aggressive when they sense prey. Some zombies can run and go around small obstacles. But they typically cannot open doors.

Zombies usually move and hunt in large mobs. They are more dangerous in groups than they are by themselves. This can make killing them very hard. Working in groups makes it easier for zombies to get human flesh. It also makes it easier for them to bite people and create more zombies.

ZOMBIE ORIGINS

The word *zombie* originally comes from Haitian and voodoo folklore. But legends of undead creatures exist all over the world. Flesh-eating monsters exist in Norse, Chinese, Arabian, and English mythology. The idea of the modern zombie is very popular in Europe and North America.

Today, zombies appear throughout popular culture.

Zombies are often connected with the apocalypse. They may signal the end of the world. Sometimes in pop culture, zombies will show up due to supernatural events. In other cases, a virus or disease might create them. Zombies bite people to spread the

FROM THE GRAVE

The Ancient Greeks may have also feared people coming back to life. Some ancient Greek graves have been dug up. These graves contained skeletons that were pinned down. The skeletons had rocks placed on top of them. Some think these rocks were there to stop the bodies from coming back to life.

Most zombies are not smart enough to open doors or get around big obstacles.

disease and make new zombies. SYFY writer Cassidy Ward explains that when someone is bitten, "the virus travels from the bite location to the brain by traveling along the nerves."[1] The sickness can infect people very quickly. There is little that can be done to stop it from spreading.

The term *zombie* has even become a **metaphor** for certain behaviors. Medical history expert Maria Cohut says that *zombie* can "refer to anyone or anything . . . that moves slowly, and demonstrates little awareness of their surroundings."[2] People who feel very tired may say they feel like a zombie. Zombies can also serve as metaphors for different fears or ideas. In some ways, zombies represent humans' fear of death itself.

2

THE HISTORY OF ZOMBIES

In the 1600s CE, many West African people were kidnapped and shipped to a French colony in Haiti. They were enslaved and forced to work on sugarcane **plantations**. The work was extremely tough. Many enslaved people died from being overworked.

The West African people brought their religious beliefs with them to Haiti. But they were also influenced by French Catholicism. The French forced enslaved people to become Catholic. This created a mixed religion known as voodoo. The idea

The original stories about zombies came from the island nation of Haiti.

of zombielike creatures came from the voodoo religion.

Enslaved people believed they would be sent back to Africa in the afterlife. They thought the only way to become truly free was through death. However, legend said people who died by suicide would not be free in the afterlife. Instead, they would

MUMMY OR ZOMBIE?

Mummies and zombies are two monsters that often get confused. They are both walking corpses. But mummies do not feed on people. They are also not **reanimated** by an infection or voodoo priest. A mummy may come back to life through a curse. Its purpose is to protect a place or an object.

become undead slaves. They would be forced to work on plantations forever. They would become a creature called a zombi.

THE HAITIAN REVOLUTION

In 1791, the enslaved people of Haiti rebelled. They overthrew slaveholders. This was known as the Haitian Revolution. People who were once enslaved took power. In 1804, Haiti became the first independent Black republic. It was a huge achievement for slaves to beat a powerful country. The revolution ended French colonialism in Haiti for good.

After the Haitian Revolution ended in 1804, the voodoo religion helped influence the zombi myth.

The myth of the zombi changed after the Haitian Revolution. It became a part of the voodoo religion. *Zombi* was a term for ghosts or spirits. They were scary creatures that could take different forms. But Haitians also believed zombis could be created by voodoo priests.

A voodoo priest was known as a bokor. People believed the bokors could bring corpses back from the dead. They did this through magic, hypnosis, or potions. Once reanimated, the corpses would become slaves to the bokor. This was because their souls had been captured. The undead would have to carry out the priest's wishes.

THE LEGEND SPREADS

In 1929, a man named William Seabrook published a book called *The Magic Island*.

It was all about Haiti and voodoo. The book describes the idea of zombies. Seabrook wrote, "The zombie, they say, is a soulless human corpse, still dead, but taken from the grave and endowed by sorcery with a mechanical semblance of life."[3] The use of the word *zombie* started to become popular after Seabrook's book was released.

American author Zora Neale Hurston also wanted to learn more about Haitian customs and zombies. She traveled to Haiti in 1937 to do research for a book. While there, Hurston saw someone who people claimed was a zombie. In an interview, she

In Zora Neale Hurston's book Tell My Horse, *Hurston describes her experiences in Haiti, including learning about voodoo and myths.*

described zombies as "people who die and

are resurrected, but without their souls.

They can take orders, and they're supposed

to never be tired, and to do what the

master says."[4]

NIGHT OF THE LIVING DEAD

One film changed how people thought

of zombies. That film was *Night of the*

Living Dead, by George A. Romero. It was

WHITE ZOMBIE

The book *The Magic Island* inspired a movie called *White Zombie*. It was a horror film released in 1932. In the movie, a couple is supposed to get married on a Haitian plantation. But the bride is given a zombie potion by a voodoo priest. The potion turns the bride into a zombie slave.

released in 1968. Romero's film is where

the modern version of a zombie comes

from. The film featured undead corpses that

hungered for human flesh.

The movie begins with people dead in a

graveyard. They become undead monsters.

These creatures then attack people hiding

out in a farmhouse. Romero's film did not

have any voodoo priests. It did not even use

the word *zombie*. But his idea of an undead

monster stuck.

Romero created several more zombie

movies. He has been called the creator of

the modern zombie genre. Romero said,

Many zombie stories are about people fighting zombies or surviving a zombie apocalypse rather than about the undead creatures themselves.

"I . . . have always liked the monster within idea. I like the zombies being us."[5] Zombies stayed popular after the release of Romero's films. And stories about zombies continue to interest audiences today.

Many people forgot the Haitian origins of zombies. Americans put their own spin on these creatures. They were no longer known as soulless slaves cursed to work forever. Instead, they became mindless, flesh-eating monsters.

3

LOOKING AT THE EVIDENCE

There is no evidence for the kind of zombies that appear in movies. Undead people do not walk around grunting with missing limbs. But some people have claimed to see zombies. There are even some cases of people and animals with zombielike symptoms.

ZOMBIE POWDER

The legend of zombies came from Haitian

voodoo culture. Some modern stories

of zombies have come from Haiti. A few

people even claim they were brought back

Sometimes a scratch from a zombie can also infect a person with the zombie virus.

from the dead as zombies. One of them is a man named Clairvius Narcisse.

Narcisse supposedly died in a Haitian hospital in 1962. He even had a death certificate. But he walked back into a small village in 1980. He approached a woman named Angelina Narcisse. He claimed that he was her brother. The man knew things that only the real Clairvius Narcisse would know. He remembered being put into the grave. But he could not speak or move while it happened. Narcisse said a voodoo priest came and raised him out of his grave. The priest made him work at a sugar

Zombies do not feel pain like people do. Missing body parts or limbs do not stop zombies from trying to get to human flesh.

plantation for twenty years. Narcisse says

he was made into a zombie slave.

A scientist named Wade Davis heard

about this story. He decided to travel to

Haiti after he heard about it. Davis wanted to learn if zombies were real. He also wanted to know how they were made. Davis studied Haitian culture. He learned that voodoo priests used powders in their rituals. Davis tested these powders. He discovered that they were made from puffer fish.

Puffer fish have a deadly **toxin** inside them. It can cause people to have zombielike symptoms. These include confusion and trouble breathing or walking. The toxin can even cause paralysis and death. It was this toxin that made people

Puffer fish toxin is called tetrodotoxin. A few other kinds of fish and some amphibian, octopus, and shellfish species also have this toxin.

appear to be dead. Davis believed Narcisse

was given the toxin. This would explain why

he appeared dead to others. The effect this

powder had on people is what made many

in Haiti start believing zombies were real.

COTARD'S SYNDROME

Some mental illnesses or disorders can cause people to act like zombies. They can also sometimes make people believe they are zombies. One example is a condition called Cotard's syndrome. It is also called walking corpse syndrome. It is very rare. People with this disorder believe they are

ZOMBIE DEER

Chronic wasting disease is an infection that affects deer across the United States. It is sometimes called zombie deer disease. Symptoms of the disease include weight loss, aggression, and lack of fear. It also causes stumbling and drooling. Luckily, the disease cannot spread to humans.

dead or decomposing. They may believe parts of their bodies are missing. They also may hear voices telling them they are dead or dying.

One woman with Cotard's syndrome believed she was actually dead. She claimed she smelled like rotting flesh. She wanted to be taken to the morgue to be with other dead people. No one really knows what causes Cotard's syndrome. It may come from types of brain damage. These include brain bleeds or strokes. People with Cotard's syndrome can get better with treatment.

The zombie ant fungus takes over an ant's mind and body.

ZOMBIE ANTS

There are also cases of some animals

becoming zombies. One type of fungus

attacks carpenter ants. It is sometimes

known as zombie ant fungus. The fungus exists in the Amazon rain forest. It infects ants and takes control of their movements.

The fungus is very deadly. Science writer Ed Yong explains, "When the fungus infects a carpenter ant, it grows through the insect's body, draining it of nutrients and **hijacking** its mind."[6] Ants have no chance of surviving once they are infected. The fungus eventually makes infected ants act differently from how they normally do.

Once an ant is infected, the fungus will force the ant out of its nest. It will then make the ant climb about 10 inches (25 cm) off

Cutting off a zombie's head is one of the ways it can be killed.

the ground. This provides the perfect place

for the fungus to grow. The ant will hang

from the bottom of a leaf by its mouth.

Meanwhile, the fungus feeds on the ant.

The fungus will then start growing out of the ant's head. From there, it will spread its spores. The fungus's spores will go on to infect other ants.

Many monsters or creatures come from myths or folklore. This includes zombies. But there are zombielike creatures and conditions that are based in fact. They can be fascinating, mysterious, and frightening. But there is little evidence of humans actually turning into flesh-eating monsters.

4
THE CULTURAL IMPACT OF ZOMBIES

Zombies became an important part of popular culture after *Night of the Living Dead*. Dozens of zombie films were made starting in the 1980s. They are still popular today. Zombies appear across all kinds of media. And the zombie genre does not seem to be going anywhere.

ZOMBIE MOVIES

Most zombie movies are considered horror

movies. They often feature violence, blood,

and gore. People's fear of zombies and

death are used to tell stories. And movies

Events like zombie walks allow people to dress up and pretend they are zombies.

featuring a zombie apocalypse imagine what the end of the world could look like.

One example is the movie *World War Z*. It was released in 2013. In *World War Z*, a zombie pandemic takes place. The zombies are faster, stronger, and more dangerous than how they are usually pictured. A virus threatens to turn all humans into zombies. People bitten by a zombie are infected with the virus. The movie gained a lot of attention. It became the highest-earning zombie movie of all time.

Zombies have also been imagined in different ways. They appear in cartoons like

The zombies in the movie World War Z **climb on top of one another so they can get over high walls.**

Scooby Doo on Zombie Island. There are also funny zombie movies. The comedy *Zombieland* is about a group of people trying to survive a zombie apocalypse. The movie makes fun of the zombie movie genre. Zombies have even appeared in romantic movies. The movie *Warm Bodies* is a zombie take on William Shakespeare's play *Romeo and Juliet*. It is a story about a zombie and a human who fall in love.

ZOMBIES IN THE MEDIA

There are many examples of zombies in pop culture. Their influence is everywhere. There are zombie video games, comic books, and board games. Zombies are popular all over the world. But a few pieces of zombie media gained huge attention.

The first video game to feature zombies was called *Entombed*. It came out in 1982. A few other zombie video games followed.

Many zombie video games are about fighting zombies. They are often set in a postapocalyptic world.

But one that really increased interest in

zombies was the game *Resident Evil*. It was

released in 1996 by the company Capcom.

This video game quickly gained popularity.

It gave players a new zombie experience.

They had to fight zombies while solving

difficult puzzles. *Resident Evil* started a zombie video game trend.

Zombies also gained popularity from pop star Michael Jackson's song "Thriller." It was released in 1982. Jackson turned his entire music video into a mini horror film. The music video featured zombies crawling out of their graves. They walked the streets.

ZOMBIE WALKS

Zombie walks are events where people dress up in zombie costumes. They walk through the streets as if they were zombies. Sometimes the walks end in cemeteries. The record for the largest gathering of zombies was set in 2014. The event was in Minneapolis, Minnesota. A total of 15,458 zombies took part.

Even Jackson turned into a zombie. He performed zombielike dance moves. The "Thriller" dance became famous around the world.

A more recent way that zombies gained popularity was from a television show. That show was *The Walking Dead*. It was based on a comic book series with the same name. The show takes place after a zombie apocalypse. Zombies have taken over the world. A group of survivors fight to stay alive. The show began in 2010 and ran for eleven seasons. There were also several spin-off television series and video games.

In some zombie stories, the surviving humans will create barriers to separate themselves from the zombies.

The Walking Dead had millions of viewers. It also received many awards.

ZOMBIE PREPAREDNESS

The term *zombie apocalypse* has now become a well-known phrase. The US government has even talked about it.

The Centers for Disease Control and Prevention (CDC) helps the nation respond to dangerous diseases. In 2011, the CDC published a blog post called "Preparedness 101: Zombie Apocalypse." The funny post used the zombie theme to teach people how to prepare for real-life disasters. These emergencies included hurricanes, earthquakes, and floods.

The CDC gave many tips on surviving a zombie apocalypse. One was to create an emergency kit with items like food, water, and medicine. Another was to make an emergency plan. So far, the guide has

not been used to survive zombie attacks.
But the advice has been useful for other
disasters and emergencies.

ARE THEY REAL?

Zombies come in a variety of forms. The
zombies from Haitian folklore are different
from those in pop culture today. Scientists
have studied ways that parasites and
viruses can affect some plants and animals.
And some people have conditions that
make them believe they are zombies. Other
people like to dress up and pretend to
be zombies.

Today, zombies are some of the most well-known monsters in pop culture.

Zombies may not be real. But they do represent real human fears. People may fear death and dying. They may even fear bodies rising from the grave. According to Stanford scholar Angela Becerra Vidergar, "Zombies are important as a reflection of ourselves."[7]

GLOSSARY

decay

to rot or decompose

folklore

traditional customs, beliefs, stories, and sayings

hijacking

taking control of something or someone

metaphor

a word or phrase that represents something else

mob

a large and disorganized group with the desire to cause trouble or violence

plantations

large farms that use laborers to plant and harvest crops like coffee, sugar, and tobacco

reanimated

brought back to life

supernatural

something that cannot be explained by natural laws or science

toxin

the poison or venom inside a plant or animal

SOURCE NOTES

CHAPTER ONE: WHAT IS A ZOMBIE?

1. Cassidy Ward, "Bats, Bacteria, and Brains: The Science Behind a Zombie Outbreak," *SYFY*, October 20, 2021. www.syfy.com.

2. Maria Cohut, "What Are the Real Zombies?" *Medical News Today*, October 31, 2019. www.medicalnewstoday.com.

CHAPTER TWO: THE HISTORY OF ZOMBIES

3. William Seabrook, *The Magic Island*. New York: Harcourt, Brace and Company, 1929, p. 93. https://archive.org.

4. Quoted in Lakshmi Gandhi, "Zoinks! Tracing the History of 'Zombie' from Haiti to the CDC," *NPR*, December 15, 2013. www.npr.org.

5. Quoted in Dave Anthony and Craig Houston, *Call of the Dead*. Activision, 2011.

CHAPTER THREE: LOOKING AT THE EVIDENCE

6. Eric Young, "How the Zombie Fungus Takes Over Ants' Bodies to Control Their Minds," *Atlantic*, November 14, 2017. www.theatlantic.com.

CHAPTER FOUR: THE CULTURAL IMPACT OF ZOMBIES

7. Quoted in Stephanie Pappas, "Why We're Obsessed with the Zombie Apocalypse," *Live Science*, February 20, 2013. www.livescience.com.

FOR FURTHER RESEARCH

BOOKS

Bradley Cole, *Zombies*. North Mankato, MN: Capstone Press, 2019.

Marty Erickson, *Zombies*. North Mankato, MN: The Child's World, 2022.

Walt K. Moon, *Zombies*. San Diego, CA: BrightPoint Press, 2022.

INTERNET SOURCES

"7 Steps to Surviving an Apocalypse (According to Science!)," *National Geographic Kids*, n.d. www.natgeokids.com.

Marguerite Johnson, "Curious Kids: Are Zombies Real?" *Conversation*, July 11, 2017. https://theconversation.com.

Jeffrey Mantz, "8 Things Everyone Needs to Know About Zombies," *NPR*, October 31, 2010. www.npr.org.

WEBSITES

Mythology.net
https://mythology.net

The Mythology.net site features information on mythical creatures throughout the world, including zombies and the undead. The site discusses the characteristics, origins, and cultural influences of the different mythical creatures.

Zombie
https://kids.britannica.com/kids/article/zombie/600661

The Britannica Kids article on zombies includes information such as definitions, legends, and origins. It aims to educate and provide resources for further learning.

Zombie Survival Guide: Survival Information
https://libguides.library.albany.edu/zombies/home

The University Libraries from the State University of New York Albany lets kids create their own zombie survival guides. It also teaches kids about good research skills.

INDEX

IMAGE CREDITS

ABOUT THE AUTHOR

Emma Kaiser is a writer and educator based in western Minnesota. She has an MFA (master of fine arts) in creative writing from the University of Minnesota, and her writing has been published in a number of magazines and publications. She is the author of three other nonfiction books for students.